Editors: Ann Redpath, Etienne Delessert
Art Director: Rita Marshall
Publisher: George R. Peterson, Jr.

Copyright © 1984 Creative Education, Inc., 123 S. Broad Street,
Mankato, Minnesota 56001, USA. American Edition.
Copyright © 1984 Grasset & Fasquelle, Paris – Editions 24 Heures, Lausanne. French Edition.
International copyrights reserved in all countries.

Library of Congress Catalog Card No.: 83-71188
Grimm, Jakob and Wilhelm; The Three Feathers
Mankato, MN: Creative Education, Inc.; 32 pages. ISBN: 0-87191-941-9

Printed in Switzerland by Imprimeries Réunies S.A. Lausanne.

THE THREE FEATHERS

JAKOB & WILHELM GRIMM
illustrated by
ELEONORE SCHMID

CREATIVE EDUCATION INC.

ONCE UPON A TIME

THERE lived a king who had three sons, two of whom were bright youths, but the youngest never had anything to say for himself. So he was called a simpleton by everyone.

Years went on, and the King felt himself growing old. He thought it was time to decide which of his sons was to succeed him.

This was not so easy, so he told the youths that whoever should bring him the most beautiful carpet should be his heir. Lest they should all want to go in the same direction and quarrel, he went up to the roof of the palace and blew three feathers up into the air, saying:

"As they fly, thither shall you follow."

One feather flew east, another west, and the third went in a straight line between the two for a little way, and then fell suddenly to the ground.

So one brother went east, and another west, and poor Dummling was left to follow the third feather which had gone no distance at all. This made his brothers much amused.

Dummling sat down beside his feather, feeling very sad and doleful. He was just thinking that all chance of the kingdom was at an end for him, when he discovered that all the time he was staring at a trapdoor in the ground.

He lifted it and found steps leading down into the earth, so he went down the stairs till he came to a door, and then he knocked.

Immediately he heard a voice singing:

"Little toad, so green and cold,
I prithee open and behold
Who it is that knocks so bold."

And the door opened, and he saw a large toad squatting in the middle of a circle of little ones. The big one bowed to him as he entered, and asked him what he sought.

"Please," said Dummling, taking off his cap and returning the bow, "I want to know if you can help me to get the most beautiful carpet in the world."

The Toad rolled her eyes for a minute, and then, turning to one of the little ones at her side, said:

"Go bring me the big casket." And the little toad hopped away, and came back dragging a large box.

Then the Toad took a key that hung around her neck on a chain, and opened the box. She drew forth the most beautiful carpet that was ever seen.

Dummling was delighted
with it. And thanking her very
heartily, he hurried up the
steps, eager to take it to the
palace.

Meanwhile, the two brothers,
never thinking that Dummling
was clever enough to find any
sort of carpet at all, said to
themselves:

"Let us buy the shawl of the
first peasant woman we meet.
That should be good enough
to win us the kingdom."

So they bought a common
old shawl at the first oppor-
tunity, and took it home to the
palace. They arrived just at the
same moment as Dummling.

The King was astonished
when the carpets were spread
out before him and he saw the
lovely thing Dummling had
brought.

"The prize," said he, "should
by rights belong to my youngest
son."

But the others were so angry
at this, and complained to
their father so much, that for
peace he had to consent to a
new test.

So the King decreed that
whoever should bring him the
most beautiful ring should be
King when he died. Then he
blew up the feathers as before,
and bade the youths follow
them.

The two eldest went east
and west, but Dummling's
feather did as it did the first
time. It fell to earth just by the
trapdoor. So he pulled it up
once again and went down
the steps.

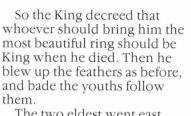

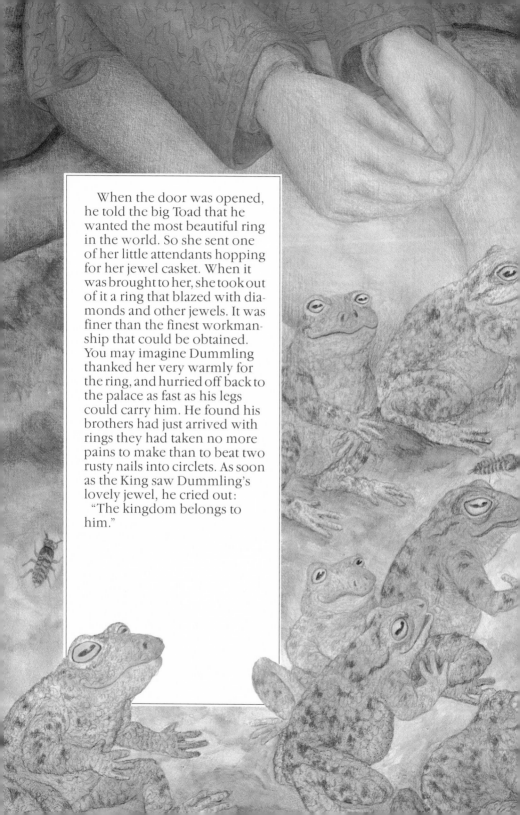

When the door was opened,
he told the big Toad that he
wanted the most beautiful ring
in the world. So she sent one
of her little attendants hopping
for her jewel casket. When it
was brought to her, she took out
of it a ring that blazed with dia-
monds and other jewels. It was
finer than the finest workman-
ship that could be obtained.
You may imagine Dummling
thanked her very warmly for
the ring, and hurried off back to
the palace as fast as his legs
could carry him. He found his
brothers had just arrived with
rings they had taken no more
pains to make than to beat two
rusty nails into circlets. As soon
as the King saw Dummling's
lovely jewel, he cried out:
  "The kingdom belongs to
him."

But the brothers again flew into a passion at this, and said that a youth who had as little wit as Dummling could not possibly reign over the land. So they complained to the father at last to make just one more condition. So this time he said that whoever should bring home the most beautiful woman in the world should succeed to the throne. A third time he blew the feathers into the air, and the youths set out after them.

Dummling's feather floated and fell just as before, and again he pulled up his trapdoor and went down into the presence of the old Toad, and told her that this time he wanted the most beautiful maiden in all the world.

"Hum!" said the Toad, "it is not everyone who gets that; still I will do my best for you, nevertheless. But first take this." And she gave Dummling a little toy cart made of a hollow carrot, to which were harnessed six beautiful white mice.

The youth looked at this rather doubtfully, and asked the Toad what he was to do with it.

"I will tell you," she said. "Take one of my little toad attendants and set her on the carrot."

So Dummling picked up the one that happened to be nearest him and put her on the carrot. Then lo and behold!

No sooner was she seated than she changed into a beautiful maiden. And the carrot and the mice were changed into a grand chariot drawn by six prancing horses. As soon as he could stop rubbing his eyes from wonder, Dummling kissed the maiden, and he drove off in triumph to the palace.

Meanwhile, the brothers, as usual, had taken no trouble whatever. At the moment Dummling drove up in his glory, they appeared with two peasant girls, who were not even pretty.

Of course the King had nothing to say but to award the kingdom to his youngest son. Of course, the elder brothers still grumbled, and made such a fuss that at last the poor King had to consent to yet another trial.

To prove which was the best wife of the three, the King decided that they should all jump through a hoop in the hall, and the one who did it most prettily was to be the winner.

And now all the court was gathered together in the hall to see the contest. The country girls jumped, but were so plump that they fell heavily and broke their arms and legs. Then Dummling's lovely maiden sprang lightly and gracefully through the ring, and landed safely on the other side.

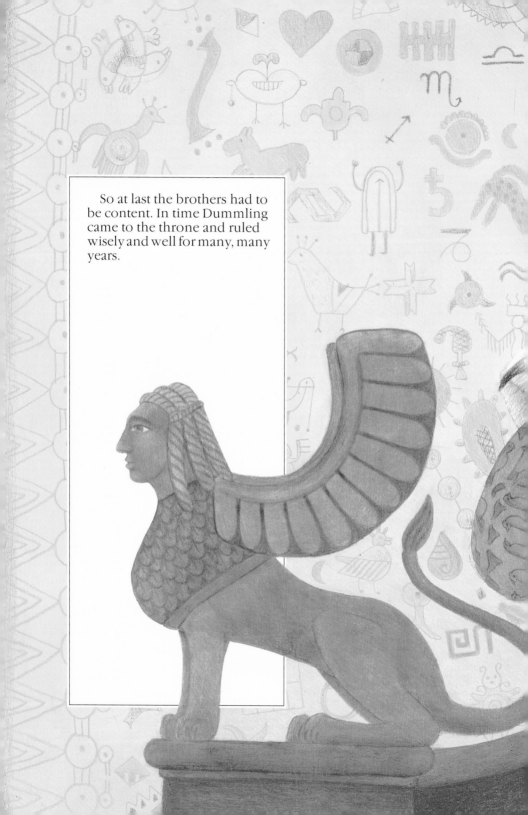

So at last the brothers had to
be content. In time Dummling
came to the throne and ruled
wisely and well for many, many
years.